Anonymous

One Hundred Progressive Hymns

Anonymous

One Hundred Progressive Hymns

ISBN/EAN: 9783337089634

Printed in Europe, USA, Canada, Australia, Japan

Cover: Foto ©Andreas Hilbeck / pixelio.de

More available books at **www.hansebooks.com**

ONE HUNDRED

PROGRESSIVE

HYMNS.

PHILADELPHIA.

1860.

The design of the compiler of these hymns in their choice and arrangement, has been to place them in the succession which has been deemed best for their study.

The first thirty will be found suitable for very young children; while a similar number at the end of the volume, will only suit those of more mature and thoughtful minds.

The large type, it is hoped, will be found as useful to parents, whose eyesight is beginning to fail, as to the very young, whose sight is often prematurely taxed by the small print of the usual editions.

HYMNS.

The Goodness of God.   C. M.

1 How kind in all his works and ways
   Must our Creator be ;
We learn some lesson of his praise
   From everything we see.

2 The glorious sun that blazes high,
   The moon more pale and dim,
With all the stars that fill the sky,
   Are made and ruled by him.

3 And this vast world of ours below,
   The water and the land,
And all the trees and flowers that grow
   Were fashioned by his hand.

4 Yes, and he formed our infant race,
   And he is ever near
To those who early seek his face
   By humble, earnest prayer.

2. *God made all things.* L. M.

1 'Twas God who made the earth and skies,
   Great are the wonders of his hand,
He is more powerful, good and wise,
   Than any child can understand.

2 Bright angels bow before his face,
   And saints stand waiting round his throne,
And in that happy, holy place,
   No sinful thoughts or words are known.

3. *The works of God.* C. M.

1 I LOVE to see the glowing sun
   Light up the deep blue sky,
Along the pleasant fields to run,
   And hear the brook flow by.

2 How fresh and green the trees appear
   What blooming flowers I find!
Oh, surely God has sent them here
   To tell us he is kind.

3 The beasts that on the herbage feed,
   Thank him in different ways;
And little birds upon the boughs
   Sing sweetly to his praise.

4 Shall I alone forget to thank
    The God who made us all?
O no, I'll humbly kneel to him
    And on my Maker call.

5 Though I am but a little child,
    Yet I to God belong;
His works declare him good and mild,
    And he will hear my song.

4.   *Who shall live in Heaven.*   S. M.

1 THERE is a land above,
    All beautiful and bright,
And those who love and seek the Lord
    Rise to that world of light.

2   There sin is known no more,
    Nor tears, nor want, nor care;
There good and happy beings dwell,
    And all are holy there.

5.   *For Morning and Evening.*   7's.

1 GRACIOUS God! to thee I pray,
    Give me grace to pray aright,
Guide and bless me every day,
    And defend me every night.

2 Let thy mercy, while I live,
    Every needful want supply;
  And thy blissful presence give,
    To support me when I die.

6.   *God's Works.*   P. M.

1 THE moon is very fair and bright,
    And also very high;
  I think it is a pretty sight
    To see it in the sky:
  It shone upon me as I lay,
  And seemed almost as bright as day.

2 The stars are very pretty too,
    And scattered all about;
  At first there seems a very few,
    But soon the rest come out:
  I'm sure I could not count them all,
  They are so very bright and small.

3 God made and keeps them, every one,
    By his great power and might:
  He is more glorious than the sun
    And all the stars of light:
  Yet though so great, we by his grace,
  If pure in heart shall see his face.

7.   *Brotherly Love.*   L. M.

1 THE God of heaven is pleased to see
  A little family agree;
  And will not slight the praise they bring,
  When loving children join to sing.

2 The gentle child that tries to please,
  That hates to quarrel, fret, and tease,
  And would not say an angry word;
  That child is pleasing to the Lord.

3 Great God! forgive, whenever we
  Forget thy will, and disagree;
  And grant that each of us may find
  The sweet delight of being kind.

8.   *Child's Prayer.*   7's.

1 JESUS, Saviour, Son of God,
  Who, for me, life's pathway trod,
  Who, for me, became a child;
  Make me humble, meek and mild.

2 I thy little lamb would be,
  Jesus, I would follow thee;
  Samuel was thy child of old,
  Take me, too, within thy fold.

9.   *The Child's Prayer.*   7's.

1 JESUS, see a little child
     Humbly at thy footstool stay;
Thou who art so meek and mild,
     Stoop, and teach me what to say.

2 Though thou art so great and high,
     Thou dost view, with smiling face,
Little children when they cry,
     " Saviour! guide us by thy grace."

3 Show me what I ought to be,
     Make me every evil shun;
Thee in all things may I see,
     In thy holy footsteps run.

4 Jesus! all my sins forgive,
     Make me lowly, pure in heart,
For thy glory may I live,
     Then be with thee where thou art.

10.   *God hears, sees, and knows me.*   C. M.

1 GOD is in heaven—can he hear
     A feeble prayer like mine?
Yes, little child, thou need'st not fear,
     He listeneth to thine.

2 God is in heaven—can he see
    When I am doing wrong?
  Yes, that he can—he looks at thee
    All day and all night long.

3 God is in heaven—would he know
    If I should tell a lie?
  Yes, if thou saidst it very low
    He'd hear it in the sky.

4 God is in heaven—can I go
    To thank him for his care?
  Not yet—but love him here below,
    And thou shalt praise him there.

11.   *The Lord is here.*   L. M.

1 THE Lord is here! He sees us too,
  And watches everything we do;
  He sees us when we laugh and play,
  And knows if we pretend to pray.

2 The Lord is here! O let us be
  Afraid to sin, for God can see;
  Lest we should be cast down to hell,
  And there in endless sorrow dwell.

12.   *God our Heavenly Father.*   L. M.

1 GREAT God! and wilt thou be so kind,
The comfort of a child to mind?
I a poor child, and thou so high,
The Lord of earth, and air, and sky?

2 Art thou my Father? canst thou hear
My feeble and imperfect prayer?
Or wilt thou listen to the praise
That such a one as I can raise?

3 Art thou my Father? let me be
A meek, obedient child to thee;
And try, in word, and deed, and thought,
To serve and please thee as I ought.

4 Art thou my Father? I'll depend
Upon the care of such a friend;
And only wish to do and be
Whatever seemeth good to thee.

5 Art thou my Father? then at last,
When all my days on earth are past,
Send down and take me in thy love,
To be thy better child above.   •

13.   *Obedience.*   C. M.

1 O THAT it were my chief delight
To do the things I ought!

Then let me try with all my might,
    To mind what I am taught.

2 Wherever I am told to go,
    I'll cheerfully obey;
Nor will I mind it much, although
    I leave a pretty play.

3 When I am bid, I'll freely bring
    Whatever I have got;
And never touch a pretty thing
    If mother tells me not.

4 And when I learn my hymns to say,
    And work, and read, and spell,
I will not think about my play,
    But try and do it well.

5 For God looks down from heaven on high,
    Our actions to behold;
And he is pleased when children try
    To do as they are told.

14.   *The Good Shepherd.*   8, 7.

1 JESUS says that we must love him;
    Helpless as the lambs are we;
But he very kindly tells us,
    That our Shepherd he will be.

2 Heavenly Shepherd, please to watch us,
      Guard us both by night and day;
  Pity show to little children,
      Who like lambs too often stray.

3 We are always prone to wander,
      Please to keep us from each snare;
  Teach our infant hearts to praise thee
      For thy kindness and thy care.

15.   *Bible Examples.*   C. M.

1 Isaac was ransomed while he lay
      Upon the altar bound;
  Moses, an infant cast away,
      Pharaoh's own daughter found.

2 Joseph, by his false brethren sold,
      God raised above them all;
  To Hannah's child the Lord foretold
      How Eli's house must fall.

3 David the bear and lion slew,
      And on Goliath trod;
  Josiah, from his boyhood knew
      His Father, David's God.

4 Children are thus Jehovah's care,
    Thus youth may seek his face;
  Since his own Son he did not spare,
    With him he gives all grace.

16.   *A Child's Prayer.*   C. M.

1 Lord, teach a sinful child to pray,
    And then accept my prayer;
  For thou canst hear the words I say,
    For thou art everywhere.

2 A little sparrow cannot fall
    Unnoticed, Lord, by thee;
  And though I am so young and small,
    Thou dost take care of me.

3 Teach me to do the thing that's right,
    And when I sin, forgive;
  And make it still my chief delight
    To serve thee while I live.

4 Whatever trouble I am in,
    To thee for help I'll call;
  But keep me, more than all, from sin,
    For that's the worst of all.

17.   *The Golden Rule.*   C. M.

1 To do to others as I would
    That they should do to me;
  Will make me honest, kind and good,
    As children ought to be.

2 I know I should not steal, nor use
    The smallest thing I see;
  Which I should never like to lose,
    If it belonged to me.

3 And this plain rule forbids me quite,
    To strike an angry blow;
  Because I should not think it right
    If others served me so.

4 But any kindness they may need,
    I'll do, whate'er it be;
  As I am very glad indeed,
    When they are kind to me.

18.   *His name is God.*   L. M.

1 WHEN I look up to yonder sky,
  So pure, so bright, so wondrous high,
  I think of One I cannot see,
  But One who sees and cares for me.

2 His name is God! he gave me birth;
  And every living thing on earth,
  And every tree and plant that grows,
  To the same hand its being owes.

3 'Tis he my daily food provides,
  And all that I require besides;
  And when I close my slumbering eye
  I sleep in peace, for he is nigh.

4 Then surely I should ever love
  This gracious God who reigns above;
  For very kind indeed is he,
  To love a little child like me.

19.   *I am the creature of God.*   L. M.

1 I am the creature of the Lord;
  He made me by his powerful word;
  This body, in each curious part,
  Was formed by his unerring art.

2 From him my nobler spirit came,
  My soul, a spark of heavenly flame.
  That soul, by which my body lives,
  Which thinks and hopes, desires and grieves,

3 Is capable of endless bliss,
  And worth a thousand worlds like this;

2

It must in heaven or hell remain,
When flesh is turned to dust again.

4 To what then should I first attend?
  Or what esteem my noblest end?
· Surely it must be this alone,
  That God my Maker may be known:

5 So known, that I may love him still,
  And form my actions by his will;
  That he may bless me while I live,
  And when I die my soul receive.

6 Then in the world of light and love,
  With saints and angel-hosts above,
  I'll dwell forever in his sight,
  In perfect knowledge and delight.

20.   *God's Greatness.*   C. M.

1 O LORD, our God, how wondrous great,
      Is thine exalted name!
  The glories of thy heavenly state
      Let old and young proclaim.

2 When I behold thy works on high,
      The moon that rules the night,
  And stars that well adorn the sky,
      Those moving worlds of light;—

3 Lord, what is man, or all his race,
    That dwells so far below,
That thou should'st visit him with grace,
    And raise his nature so!

4 O Lord, our Lord, how wondrous great
    Is thine exalted name!
The glories of thy heavenly state
    Let all the earth proclaim.

21.   *God is glorious.*   C. M.

1 How glorious is our heavenly King,
    Who reigns above the sky?
How shall a child presume to sing
    His dreadful majesty?

2 How great his power, none can tell,
    Nor think how large his grace;
Not men below, nor saints that dwell
    On high before his face.

3 Not angels that stand round the Lord
    Can search his secret will;
But they perform his holy word,
    And sing his praises still.

4 Then let me join this heavenly train,
   And my first offerings bring;
 The God of grace will not disdain
   To hear an infant sing.

22.   *True Wisdom.*   S. M.

1   King Solomon of old
     A happy choice had made;
 'Twas not for life, 'twas not for gold,
     Nor honours that he prayed.

2   He chose the better part;
     He sought for purer joys;
 A wise and understanding heart;
     And God approved his choice.

3   Far better than his crown,
     And all his grand array,
 That wisdom was, which God sent down
     To guide him on his way.

23.   *Remember now thy Creator.*   C. M.

1 Remember thy Creator now,
     In these thy youthful days;
 He will accept thine earliest vow;
     He loves thine earliest praise.

2 Remember thy Creator now,
    Seek him while he is near;
For evil days will come when thou
    Shalt find no comfort here.

3 Remember thy Creator now,
    His willing servant be;
Then, when thy head in death shall bow,
    He will remember thee.

4 Almighty God! our hearts incline
    Thy heavenly voice to hear;
Let all our future days be thine,
    Devoted to thy fear.

24.   *The object of our Creation.*   L. M.

1 WHY have we lips, if not to sing
The praises of our heavenly King?
Why have we hearts, if not to love
Our Father and our Friend above?

2 Why were our curious bodies made,
And every part in order laid?
Why, but that each of us might stand
A living wonder from his hand?

3 Why have we souls, if not to know
The God from whom our mercies flow?

Sure this can never be our lot,
Like senseless brutes, to know Him not!

4 Why have we life?—if not to gain
Immortal life, 'tis worse than vain:
This is the end for which 'twas given,—
We live on earth, to live in heaven.

5 Why did the Saviour leave the sky,
Hang on a cross, and bleed, and die?
And why are kind persuasions sent
To call and win us to repent?

6 Surely it is—that robed in white,
And made well-pleasing in his sight,
Our souls may join the happy throng,
And sing the everlasting song.

25. *Sincerity in Prayer.* C. M.

1 WHEN daily I kneel down to pray,
  As I am taught to do,
God does not care for what I say
  Unless I feel it too.

2 Yet foolish thoughts my heart beguile;
  And when I pray or sing,
I'm often thinking all the while
  About some other thing.

3 O let me never, never dare
    To act a trifler's part,
  Or think that God will hear a prayer
    That comes not from the heart.

4 But if I make his ways my choice,
    As holy children do,
  Then, while I seek him with my voice,
    My heart will love him too.

26. *Against Pride in Clothes.* L. M.

1 How proud are we, how fond to show
  Our clothes, and call them rich and new;
  When the poor sheep and silk-worms wore,
  That very clothing long before!

2 The tulip and the butterfly
  Appear in gayer coats than I:
  Let me be drest fine as I will,
  Flies, worms, and flowers exceed me still.

3 Then will I set my heart to find
  Inward adornings of the mind;
  Knowledge and virtue, truth and grace,
  These are the robes of richest dress.

4 No more shall worms with me compare;
This is the raiment angels wear;
The Son of God, when here below
Put on this bless'd apparel too.

5 In this, on earth, would I appear,
Then go to heaven, and wear it there;
God will approve it in his sight;
'Tis his own work, and his delight.

27. *The Creator praised in his Works.* L. M.

1 THE spacious firmament on high,
With all the blue ethereal sky,
And spangled heavens, a shining frame,
Their great Original proclaim.

2 The unwearied sun, from day to day,
Does his Creator's power display,
And publishes to every land
The work of an Almighty hand.

3 Soon as the evening shades prevail,
The moon takes up the wondrous tale;
And nightly, to the listening earth,
Repeats the story of her birth;

4 While all the stars that round her burn
And all the planets in their turn,

Confirm the tidings as they roll,
And spread the truth from pole to pole.

5 What though in solemn silence all
Move round this dark terrestrial ball;
What though no real voice nor sound
Amidst their radiant orbs be found;

6 In reason's ear they all rejoice,
And utter forth a glorious voice,
For ever singing as they shine,
" The hand that made us is divine."

28.   *There is a God.*   L. M.

1 THERE is a God who reigns above,
The Lord of heaven, and earth, and seas,
I fear his wrath, I ask his love,
And with my lips I sing his praise.

2 There is a law which he hath made,
To teach us all what we must do;
And his commands must be obeyed,
For they are holy, just and true.

3 There is an hour when I must die;
Nor do I know how soon 'twill come;
Thousands of children young as I
Are called by death to hear their doom.

4 Let me improve the hours I have,
　　Before the day of grace is fled,
There's no repentance in the grave,
　　Nor pardon offered to the dead.

29. *Children Mocking.* C. M.

1 OUR tongues were made to bless the Lord,
　　And not to speak ill of men;
When others give a railing word,
　　We must not rail again.

2 Should any dare to be profane,
　　To mock, and jeer, and scoff
At holy things, or holy men,
　　The Lord shall cut them off.

30. *Allurements of Sin.* 7's.

1 MANY voices seem to say,
"Hither, children—here's the way,
Haste along, and nothing fear,
Every pleasant thing is here!"

2 Yes—but whither would ye lead?
Is it happiness indeed?
Or a little shining show,
Leading down to death and woe?

3 We were made for better things;
 High as heaven our nature springs;
 Like the lark that upward flies,
 We were made to seek the skies.

4 We were made to love and fear
 That great God who placed us here,
 Made to study and fulfill
 All his good and holy will.

5 We were made to work awhile,
 Cheerful at our work to smile:
 Thinking, as we labour thus,
 Of the heaven prepared for us.

6 So, a pleasant path we'll tread,
 By the hand of Jesus led;
 Till, from sin and sorrow freed,
 Ours is happiness indeed!

31.   *The Child's Hymn.*   7's.

1 POOR and needy though I be,
 God, my Maker, cares for me;
 Gives me clothing, shelter food,
 Gives me all I have of good.

2 He will listen when I pray,
 He is with me night and day,

When I sleep and when I wake,
Keeps me safe for Jesus' sake.

3 He who reigns above the sky,
Once became as poor as I;
He whose blood for me was shed,
Had not where to lay his head.

4 Though I labor here awhile,
He will bless me with his smile;
And when this short life is past,
I shall rest with him at last.

32. *What the Bible tells us.* L. M.

1 THIS is a precious book indeed;
Happy the child that loves to read;
'Tis God's own word, which he hath given
To show our souls the way to heaven.

2 It tells us how the world was made;
And how good men the Lord obeyed;
And his commands are in it too,
To teach us what we ought to do.

3 It bids us all from sin to fly,
Because our souls can never die:
It points to heaven, where angels dwell,
And warns us to escape from hell.

4 But what is more than all beside,
  The Bible tells us, Jesus died;
  This is its first, its chief intent,
  To lead poor sinners to repent.

5 Let us be thankful that we may
  Read this good Bible every day;
  And learn the way that God hath given,
  To lead our souls to peace and heaven.

33. *Duty to Parents.* C. M.

1 LET children that would fear the Lord
     Hear what their teachers say,
  With reverence heed their parents' word,
     And with delight obey.

2 Have we not heard what dreadful plagues
     Are threatened by the Lord,
  To him who breaks his father's law,
     Or mocks his mother's word?

3 But those who worship God, and give
     Their parents honour due,
  Shall long on earth in comfort live,
     And live hereafter too.

34.   *Humility and Love of Christ.*   C. M.

1 WHEN Jesus left his Father's throne,
    He chose an humble birth;
And all unhonoured and unknown,
    He came to dwell on earth.

2 Like him may we be found below,
    In wisdom's path of peace;
Like him in grace and knowledge grow,
    As years and strength increase.

3 Sweet were his words, and kind his look
    When mothers round him pressed;
Their infants in his arms he took,
    And on his bosom blessed.

4 Safe from the world's alluring charms,
    Beneath his watchful eye,
Thus in the circle of his arms
    May we for ever lie.

35.   *How to pray aright.*   S. M.

1   I OFTEN say my prayers,
        But do I ever pray?
    Or do the wishes of my heart
        Suggest the words I say?

2   'Tis useless to implore,
        Unless I feel my need :
Unless 'tis from a sense of want
        That all my prayers proceed.

3   I may as well kneel down
        And worship gods of stone
As offer to the living God
        A prayer of words alone.

4   For words without the heart
        The Lord will never hear ;
Nor will he ever those regard
        Whose prayers are insincere.

5   Lord ! teach me what I want,
        And teach me how to pray ;
Nor let me e'er implore thy grace,
        Not feeling what I say.

36.   *Early Instruction.*   C. M.

1 HAPPY the child whose early years
      Receive instruction well ;
Who hates the sinner's path, and fears
      The road that leads to hell.

2 'Twill save us from a thousand snares
      To mind religion young ;

Grace will preserve our following years,
    And make our virtues strong.

3 To thee, Almighty God, to thee
    Our childhood we resign;
'Twill please us to look back, and see
    That our whole lives were thine.

37.   *Lying.*   S. M.

1   GOD is a God of truth,
      And hates a lying tongue;
And what is more depraved in youth?
      A liar bold and young?

2   Nothing can be concealed
      By the most artful lie;
To God it is at once revealed,
      For he is ever by.

38.   L. M.

"Let the people praise thee, O God; let ALL the people praise
thee." PSALM lxvii. 3.

1 From all that dwell below the skies,
Let the Creator's praise arise;
Let the Redeemer's name be sung
Through every land, by every tongue.

2 Eternal are thy mercies, Lord,
  And truth eternal is thy Word:
  Thy praise shall sound from shore to shore,
  Till suns shall rise and set no more.

39.   *The Birth of Christ.*   C. M.

1 WHILE shepherds watched their flocks by night,
    All seated on the ground,
  The angel of the Lord came down,
    And glory shone around.

2 Fear not, said he, (for mighty dread
    Had seizéd their troubled mind,)
  Glad tidings of great joy I bring
    To you and all mankind.

3 To you, in David's town, this day,
    Is born of David's line,
  The Saviour, who is Christ the Lord;
    And this shall be the sign :

4 The heavenly babe you there shall find
    To human view displayed,
  All meanly wrapped in swathing-bands,
    And in a manger laid.

5 Thus spake the seraph, and forthwith
    Appeared a shining throng

3

Of angels praising God on high,
  Who thus addressed their song :

6 All glory be to God on high,
  And to the earth be peace ;
Good will henceforth, from heaven to men.
  Begin and never cease.

40.   *Early consecration.*   C. M.

1 IN the bright morn of life, when youth
  With vital ardour glows,
And shines in all the fairest charms
  That beauty can disclose.

2 Deep in thy soul, before its powers
  Are yet by vice enslaved,
Be thy Creator's glorious name
  And character engraved.

3 Ere yet the shades of sorrow cloud
  The sunshine of thy days ;
And cares, and toils, in endless round
  Encompass all thy ways :

4 Ere yet thy heart the woes of age
  With vain regret deplore,
And sadly muse on former joys
  That now return no more.

5 True wisdom, early sought and gained,
  In age will give thee rest;
  O then, improve the morn of life,
  To make its evening blest!

41. *Value of Religion.* 7's.

  'Tis religion that can give
  Sweetest pleasure while we live,
  'Tis religion must supply
  Solid comfort when we die.
  After death, its joys will be
  Lasting as eternity!
  Be the living God my friend,
  Then my bliss shall never end.

42. *Time is Flying.* C. M.

1 How long sometimes a day appears!
  And weeks, how long are they!
  Months move along, as if the years
  Would never pass away.

2 But months and years are passing by,
  And soon must all be gone;
  For day by day, as minutes fly,
  Eternity comes on.

3 Days, months, and years must have an end
　　Eternity has none :
　'Twill always have as long to spend
　　As when it first begun.

4 Great God, an infant cannot tell ·
　　How such a thing can be ;
　I only pray that I may dwell
　　That long, long time with thee.

43.　　　*The Guide of the Young.*　　　C. M.

1 How shall the young secure their hearts
　　And guard their lives from sin ?
　Thy word the choicest rules impart,
　　To keep the conscience clean.

2 Thy word is everlasting truth ;
　　How pure is every page !
　O may its precepts guide our youth,
　　And well support our age.

3 'Tis like the sun, a heavenly light,
　　That guides us all the day ;
　And through the dangers of the night,
　　A lamp to lead our way.

4 Lord, send thy word to every heart,
   By thine almighty voice :
Early from sin may we depart,
   And make thy love our choice.

44.   *Christ's Example.*   L. M.

1 WHENE'ER the angry passions rise,
   And tempt our thoughts or tongues to strife;
To Jesus let us lift our eyes,
   Bright pattern of the Christian life.

2 O how benevolent and kind !
   How mild and ready to forgive !
Be this the temper of our mind,
   And these the rules by which we live.

3 To do his heavenly Father's will
   Was his employment and delight :
Humility and holy zeal
   Shone through his life supremely bright.

4 But O how blind, how weak we are !
   How frail ! how apt to turn aside !
Lord ! we depend upon thy care,
   We ask thy Spirit for our guide.

5 Thy fair example may we trace,
  To teach us what we ought to be ;
Make us by thy transforming grace,
  O Saviour! daily more like thee.

45. *Jesus Christ an Example.* P. M.

1 JESUS when a little child
  Taught us what we ought to be;
Holy, harmless, undefiled,
  Was the Saviour's infancy :
All the Father's glory shone
In the person of his Son.

2 As in age and strength he grew,
  Heavenly wisdom filled his breast ;
Crowds attentive round him drew,
  Wondering at their infant guest :
Gazed upon his lovely face,
Saw him full of truth and grace.

3 In his heavenly Father's house,
  Jesus spent his early days ;
There he paid his solemn vows,
  There proclaimed his Father's praise;
Thus it was his lot to gain
Favour both with God and man.

4 Father, guide our steps aright,
    In the way that Jesus trod;
May it be our great delight
    To obey thy will, O God?
Then to us shall soon be given
Endless bliss with Christ in heaven.

46.   *Morning Hymn.*   L. M.

1 AWAKE, my soul, and with the sun
Thy daily stage of duty run;
Shake of dull sloth, and early rise,
To pay thy morning sacrifice.

2 Glory to Thee, who safe has kept,
And hast refreshed me, while I slept;
Grant, Lord, when I from death shall wake
I may of endless life partake.

3 Lord, I my vows to thee renew,
Scatter my sins as morning dew;
Guard my first springs of thought and will,
And with thyself my spirit fill.

4 Direct, control, suggest, this day,
All I design, or do, or say;
That all my powers, with all their might,
In thy sole glory may unite.

47. *The Night of Death.* S. M.

1 THE day is past and gone ;
  The evening shades appear ;
O may we all remember well
  The night of death draws near.

2 We lay our garments by,
  Upon our beds to rest ;
So death shall soon disrobe us all
  Of what we here possessed.

3 Lord, keep us safe this night,
  Secure from all our fears ;
May angels guard us while we sleep,
  Till morning light appears.

48. *The Request.* C. M.

1 FATHER, whate'er of earthly bliss
  Thy sovereign will denies,
Accepted at thy throne of grace
  Let this petition rise.

2 Let the sweet hope that thou art mine
  My life and death attend ;
Thy presence through my journey shine
  And crown my journey's end.

49. *The Heavenly Sabbath.* L. M.

1 ANOTHER six day's work is done,
Another Sabbath is begun :
Return, my soul, enjoy thy rest,
Improve the day that God hath blessed.

2 Come, bless the Lord, whose love assigns
So sweet a rest to wearied minds;
Draws us away from earth to heaven,
And gives this day the food of seven.

3 O may our prayers and praises rise
As grateful incense to the skies;
And draw from heaven that sweet repose
Which none but he who feels it knows.

4 In holy duties may the day,
In holy pleasures pass away;
How sweet a Sabbath thus to spend,
In hope of one that ne'er shall end.

50. *Omniscience.* L. M.

1 LORD, thou hast searched and seen me through,
Thine eye commands, with piercing view,
My rising and my resting hours,
My heart and flesh, with all their powers.

2 My thoughts, before they are my own,
Are to my God distinctly known;
He knows the words I mean to speak,
Ere from my opening lips they break.

3 Within thy circling power I stand;
On every side I find thy hand;
Awake, asleep, at home, abroad,
I am surrounded still with God.

4 How awful is thy searching eye!
Thy knowledge, O how deep! how high!
My soul, with all the powers I boast,
Is in the boundless prospect lost.

5 O may these thoughts possess my breast
Where'er I rove, where'er I rest;
Nor let my evil passions dare
Consent to sin, for God is there.

51.　　　*We cannot trust Liars.*　　　L. M.

1 O 'TIS a lovely thing for youth
To walk betimes in wisdom's way!
To fear a lie, to speak the truth,
That we may trust to all they say!

2 But liars we can never trust,
Though they should speak the thing that's
true;

And he that does one fault at first,
  And lies to hide it, makes it two.

3 Have children never heard, nor read,
  How God abhors deceit and wrong?
How Ananias was struck dead,
  Caught with a lie upon his tongue?

4 So did his wife Sapphira die,
  When she came in, and grew so bold
As to confirm the wicked lie,
  That, just before, her husband told.

5 The Lord delights in them that speak
  The words of truth; but every liar
Must have his portion in the lake
  That burns with brimstone and with fire.

52.   *Conscience.*   7's.

1 WHEN a foolish thought within
  Tries to take us in a snare,
Conscience tells us, "It is sin,"
  And entreats us to beware.

2 If in something we transgress,
  And are tempted to deny,
Conscience says, "Your fault confess;
  Do not dare to tell a lie."

3 In the morning, when we rise,
   And would fain omit to pray,
 " Child consider," Conscience cries,
   " Should not God be sought to-day ?"

4 When our angry passions rise,
   Tempting to revenge an ill ;
 " Now subdue it," Conscience cries,
   " And command your temper still."

5 Thus, without our will or choice,
   This good monitor within,
With a secret, gentle voice,
   Warns us to beware of sin.

6 But if we should disregard,
   While this friendly voice would call,
Conscience soon will grow so hard,
   That it will not speak at all.

53.   *Our Father in Heaven.*   11's.

1 Our Father in heaven, we hallow thy name :
May thy kingdom, all holy, on earth be the same.
O give to us daily our portion of bread :
It is from thy bounty that all must be fed.

2 Forgive our transgression, and teach us to
know
That humble compassion that pardons each
foe.
Save us from temptation, from weakness and
sin;
And thine be the glory, forever. Amen.

54. *But two Ways.* C. M.

1 THERE is a path that leads to God :
All others go astray ;
Narrow, but pleasant is the road,
And Christians love the way.

2 It leads straight through this world of sin,
And dangers must be past;
But those who boldly walk therein
Will come to heaven at last.

3 While the broad road, where thousands go,
Lies near, and opens fair;
And many turn aside, I know,
To walk with sinners there.

4 But lest my feeble steps should slide,
Or wander from thy way,
Lord, condescend to be my guide,
And I shall never stray.

55. *Happiness.* 7, 6.

1 It is not earthly pleasure,
    That withers in a day;
It is not mortal treasure,
    That flieth soon away;
It is not friends that leave us,
    It is not sense nor sin,
That smile but to deceive us,
    Can give us peace within.

2 But 'tis religion bringeth
    Joy beyond earth's control;
Rich from the throne it springeth
    A fountain to the soul;
He that is meek and lowly,
    The Saviour's face shall see;
To none but to the holy,
    Heaven's gates shall opened be.

56. *Frailty.* S. M.

1 The lilies of the field,
    That quickly fade away,
May well to us a lesson yield,
    For we are frail as they.

2 Just like an early rose,
    I've seen an infant bloom :

But death, perhaps, before it blows.
Will lay it in the tomb.

3 Then let us think on death,
    Though we are young and gay ;
For God, who gave our life and breath,
    Can take them both away.

4 To God, who made them all,
    Let children humbly cry ;
And then, whenever death may call.
    They'll be prepared to die.

57.   *Mariner's Hymn.*   L. M.

1 HAPPY is he who early steers,
    Like a trim vessel, straight for heaven ;
Who Christian colours bravely rears,
    And keeps the course that God has given.

2 Life is the ocean ; years the tide
    That floats ten thousand barks along ;
Sins are the rocks on every side
    Where passion drives a current strong.

3 Pleasure that looks so bright and fair,
    Is like the shallows, set with sands ;
And many a wreck, forlorn and bare,
    Lies high and dry upon those strands.

4 Faith is the compass, firm and true,
   Whose needle points to Christ the pole;
That morning star will guide us through,
   Though winds may howl and waves may
     roll.

58.   *The mellow Eve is gliding.*   7, 6.

1 THE mellow eve is gliding
   Serenely down the west;
So, every care subsiding,
   My soul would sink to rest.

2 The woodland hum is ringing
   The daylight's gentle close;
May angels round me singing,
   Thus hymn my last repose.

3 The evening star has lighted
   Her crystal lamp on high;
So, when in death benighted,
   May hope illume the sky.

4 In golden splendour dawning,
   The morrow's light shall break;
O! on the last bright morning,
   May I in glory wake.

59.   *Call to Praise.*   7's.

1 CHILDREN of the heavenly King,
  As we journey, sweetly sing;
  Sing our Saviour's worthy praise,
  Glorious in his works and ways.

2 We are travelling home to God
  In the way our fathers trod;
  They are happy now, and we
  Soon their happiness shall see.

3 Fear not, brethren, joyful stand
  On the borders of our land,
  Jesus Christ, our Father's Son,
  Bids us undismayed go on.

4 Lord! obediently we'll go,
  Gladly leaving all below;
  Only thou our leader be,
  And we still will follow thee.

60.   *The broad and narrow Way.*

1 STRIVE, for the way is strait
      In which the Saviour trod;
  And narrow is the gate
      That leadeth up to God.

Cut off the ensnaring hand,
    Pluck out the ensnaring eye;
Turn ye at God's command;
    Sinners, why will ye die?

2 Strive, for there are but few
    Who find the living way;
Children, alas! will you
    Still blindly go astray?
O shun the crowded gate,
    Though wide it seem, and fair,
'Twill bring you, soon or late,
    To anguish and despair.

3 Strive, ere life's setting sun
    Shall sink in thickest gloom:
Strive, night is coming on,
    Ye hasten to the tomb.
Ask; mercy shall be given;
    Seek as for hidden gold;
Knock, and the Lord of heaven
    The gates will wide unfold.

61.   *The Lord's Prayer.*   L. M.

1 OUR Father, full of grace divine,
    To thy great name be praises paid;
Thy kingdom come, thy glory shine,
    And be thy will on earth obeyed.

2 Give us our bread from day to day,
  And all our wants do thou supply;
With gospel truths feed us, we pray,
  That we may never faint or die.

3 Extend thy grace, our hearts renew,
  Our each offence in love forgive;
Teach us divine forgiveness too,
  And let us free from evil live.

4 For thine's the kingdom, and the power,
  And all the glory waits thy name;
Let every land thy grace adore,
  And sound a long and loud Amen.

62.   *For the Holy Spirit.*   L. M.

1 My Father, when I come to thee,
I would not only bend the knee,
But with my spirit seek thy face,—
With my whole heart desire thy grace.

2 I plead the name of thy dear Son;
All he has said, all he has done;
O may I feel his love for me,
Who died from sin to set me free!

3 To guide me, Lord, be ever nigh;
My sins forgive, my wants supply;

With favour crown my youthful days,
And my whole life shall bear thy praise.

4 Thy Holy Spirit, Lord, impart;
Impress thy likeness on my heart;
Let me obey thy truth in love,
'Till raised to dwell with thee above.

63.　　　*Blessings of the Godly.*　　　S. M.

1 THE man is ever blest
Who shuns the sinner's ways;
Amongst their counsels never stands,
Nor takes the scorner's place :

2 But makes the law of God
His study and delight,
Amidst the labors of the day,
And watches of the night.

3 He like a tree shall thrive,
With waters near the root;
Fresh as the leaf, his name shall live;
His works are heavenly fruit.

4 Not so the ungodly race,
They no such blessings find;
Their hopes shall flee like empty chaff
Before the driving wind.

5 How will they bear to stand
  Before that judgment-seat,
Where all the saints at Christ's right hand
  In full assembly meet.

6 He knows and he approves
  The way the righteous go ;
But sinners and their works shall meet
  A dreadful overthrow.

64. *Worship.* 11, 12.

1 O LORD, let our songs find acceptance before
      thee,
    And pierce through the skies to thine
      uppermost throne ;
  For thou stoopest to listen when mortals
      adore thee,
    And sendest thy blessings like messengers
      down.

2 Our Father, our Father, we ask thee to guide
      us,
    And keep us from sin till life's journey be
      o'er ;
  Then the last sigh of nature, whate'er else
      betide us,
    Shall waft us to glory, when time is no
      more.

3 Then, then will we sing the sweet song of
    the blessed,
  And mingle our strains with the myriads
    above;
  Far surpassing all strains that our tongues
    e'er expressed,
  And Jesus, the chorus, and Infinite Love.

65.   *The Ark.*   S. M.

1 BEHOLD the ark of God!
  Behold the open door!
Hasten to gain the blest abode,
  And rove, my soul, no more.

2 There safe shalt thou abide,
  There sweet shall be thy rest:
And every wish be satisfied,
  With full salvation blest.

3 And when the waves of wrath,
  Again the earth shall fill,
Thine ark shall ride the sea of fire,
  And rest on Zion's hill.

66.   *Love of God.*   7's.

1 SING, my soul, his wondrous love,
  Who from yon bright world above

Ever watchful o'er our race,
Still to man extends his grace :
Sing, my soul, his wondrous love.

2 Heaven and earth by him were made,
He by all must be obeyed ;
What are we, that he should show
So much love to us below !
Sing, my soul, his wondrous love.

3 God, thus merciful and good,
Bought us with a Saviour's blood,
And, to make our safety sure,
Guides us by his Spirit pure :
Sing, my soul, his wondrous love.

4 Sing, my soul, adore his name,
Let his glory be thy theme ;
Praise him till he calls thee home,
Trust his love for all to come :
Praise, O praise the God of love.

67. *God's Protection.* 8's.

1 INSPIRER and hearer of prayer,
   Thou Shepherd and guardian of thine,
My all to thy covenant care
   I, sleeping or waking, resign.

2 If thou art my shield and my sun,
    The night is no darkness to me :
And fast as my minutes roll on,
    They bring me but nearer to thee.

3 A sovereign protector I have,
    Unseen, yet forever at hand ;'
Unchangeably faithful to save,
    Almighty to rule and command.

4 His smiles and his comforts abound,
    His grace, as the dew, shall descend ;
And walls of salvation surround
    The soul he delights to defend.

68.   *God eternal.*   C. M.

1 O God! our help in ages past,
    Our hope for years to come,
Our shelter from the stormy blast,
    And our eternal home :

2 Beneath the shadow of thy throne
    Thy saints have dwelt secure ;
Sufficient is thine arm alone,
    And our defence is sure.

3 Before the hills in order stood,
    Or earth received her frame,

From everlasting thou art God,
Through endless years the same.

4 Time, like an overflowing stream,
Bears all its sons away;
We fly forgotten, as a dream
Dies at the opening day.

5 O God! our help in ages past,
Our hope for years to come,
Be thou our guard while life shall last,
And our eternal home.

69. *Heaven.* C. M.

1 THERE is a land of pure delight
Where saints immortal reign;
Infinite day excludes the night,
And pleasures banish pain.

2 There everlasting spring abides,
And never-withering flowers;
Death, like a narrow sea, divides
This heavenly land from ours.

3 Sweet fields beyond the swelling flood
Stand dressed in living green;
So to the Jews old Canaan stood,
While Jordan rolled between.

4 But timorous mortals start, and shrink
    To cross the narrow sea;
And linger, shivering on the brink,
    And fear to launch away.

5 O, could we make our doubts remove,
    Those gloomy doubts that rise;
And see the Canaan that we love,
    With unbeclouded eyes;

6 Could we but climb where Moses stood,
    And view the landscape o'er;
Not Jordan's stream, nor death's cold flood
    Should fright us from the shore.

70.   *Pressing onwards.*   C. M.

1 AWAKE, my soul! stretch every nerve
    And press with vigor on;
A heavenly race demands thy zeal,
    And an immortal crown.

2 A cloud of witnesses around,
    Hold thee in full survey;
Forget the steps already trod,
    And onward urge thy way.

3 'Tis God's all-animating voice
    That calls thee from on high ;
'Tis his own hand presents the prize
    To thine aspiring eye.

71. *What is Prayer.* C. M.

1 PRAYER is the soul's sincere desire,
    Unuttered or expressed ;
The motion of a hidden fire
    That trembles in the breast.

2 Prayer is the burden of a sigh,
    The falling of a tear ;
The upward glancing of an eye,
    When none but God is near.

3 Prayer is the simplest form of speech
    That infant lips can try ;
Prayer the sublimest strains that reach
    The majesty on high.

4 Prayer is the contrite sinner's voice
    Returning from his ways ;
While angels in their songs rejoice,
    And say,—" Behold he prays."

72. *The Benefits of Prayer.* L. M.

1 PRAYER is appointed to convey
   The blessings God designs to give ;
Long as they live should Christians pray,
   For only while they pray they live.

2 If pain afflict, or wrongs oppress ;
   If cares distract, or fears dismay ;
If guilt deject ; if sin distress ;
   In every case, still watch and pray.

3 'Tis prayer supports the soul that's weak ;
   Though thought be broken, language lame,
Pray, if thou canst, or canst not speak ;
   But pray with faith in Jesus' name.

4 Depend on him, thou canst not fail ;
   Make all thy wants and wishes known ;
Fear not, his merits must prevail ;
   Ask but in faith, it shall be done.

73. *Reliance on divine Assistance.* S. M.

1 HEIRS of unending life,
   While yet we sojourn here,
O let us our salvation work
   With trembling and with fear.

2 God will support our hearts
    With might before unknown;
The work to be performed is ours,
    The strength is all his own.

3 'Tis he that works to will,
    'Tis he that works to do;
His is the power by which we act,
    His be the glory too!

74. *Christian Warfare.* S. M.

1 SOLDIERS of Christ, arise,
    And put your armour on,
Strong in the strength which God supplies,
    Through his eternal Son;

2 Strong in the Lord of Hosts,
    And in his mighty power,
Who in the strength of Jesus trusts,
    Is more than conqueror.

3 Stand then in his great might,
    With all his strength endued;
But take, to arm you for the fight,
    The panoply of God;

4 That having all things done,
    And all your conflicts past,
Ye may o'ercome through Christ alone,
    And stand entire at last.

75.   *The Danger of Delay.*   L. M

1 HASTEN, O sinner, to be wise
    And stay not for the morrow's sun;
The longer wisdom you despise,
    The harder is she to be won.

2 O hasten mercy to implore,
    And stay not for the morrow's sun;
For fear thy season should be o'er
    Before this evening's hours are gone.

3 O hasten, sinner, to return,
    And stay not for the morrow's sun;
For fear thy lamp should cease to burn
    Before the needful work is done.

4 O hasten, sinner, to be blest,
    And stay not for the morrow's sun;
For fear the curse should thee arrest
    Before the morrow is begun.

76 *Communion with God.* L. M.

1 My God, permit me not to be
  A stranger to myself and thee;
  Amid a thousand thoughts I rove,
  Forgetful of my highest love.

2 Why should my passions mix with earth,
  And thus debase my heavenly birth?
  Why should I cleave to things below,
  And let my God, my Saviour, go?

3 Call me away from flesh and sense,
  One sovereign word can draw me thence;
  I would obey the voice divine,
  And all inferior joys resign.

77. *"It is finished."* L. M.

1 'Tis finished—so the Saviour cried,
  And meekly bowed his head and died.
  'Tis finished—yes, the work is done,
  The battle fought, the victory won.

2 'Tis finished—all that heaven decreed,
  And all the ancient prophets said,
  Is now fulfilled, as long designed,
  In me, the Saviour of mankind.

3 'Tis finished—Aaron now no more
  Must stain his robes with purple gore ;
  The sacred veil is rent in twain,
  And Jewish rites no more remain.

4 'Tis finished, this, my dying groan,
  Shall sins of every kind atone :
  Millions shall be redeemed from death
  By this, my last expiring breath.

5 'Tis finished—let the joyful sound
  Be heard through all the nations round :
  'Tis finished—let the echo fly
  Through heaven and hell, through earth and
    sky.

78.   *The Fear of Death removed.*   L. M.

1 WHY should we start and fear to die ?
    What timorous worms we mortals are ;
  Death is the gate to endless joy,
    And yet we dread to enter there.

2 The pains, the groans, the dying strife,
    Fright our approaching souls away ;
  And we shrink back again to life,
    Fond of our prison and our clay.

3 O if my Lord would come and meet,
  My soul would stretch her wings in haste,
Fly fearless through death's iron gate,
  Nor feel the terrors as she past!

4 Jesus can make a dying bed
  Feel soft as downy pillows are,
While on his breast I lean my head,
  And breathe my life out sweetly there.

79.   L. M.

"Now faith is the substance of things hoped for, the evidence of
things not seen."—HEB. xi. 1.

1 As when the weary traveler gains
  The height of some o'erlooking hill,
His heart revives, if, o'er the plains,
  He eyes his home tho' distant still:

2 So when the Christian pilgrim views,
  By faith his mansion in the skies,
The sight his fainting strength renews,
  And wings his speed to reach the prize.

3 'Tis there, he says, I am to dwell
  With Jesus in the realms of day:
Then I shall bid my cares farewell,
  And he will wipe my tears away.

5

80.   *Heaven desirable.*   11's.

1 I WOULD not live alway: I ask not to stay
  Where storm after storm rises dark o'er the
      way ;
  The few lurid mornings that dawn on us here
  Are enough for life's woes, full enough for
      its cheer.

2 I would not live alway, thus fettered by sin,
  Temptation without, and corruption within :
  E'en the rapture of pardon is mingled with
      fears,
  And the cup of thanksgiving with penitent
      tears.

3 I would not live alway; no—welcome the
      tomb ;
  Since Jesus hath lain there, I dread not its
      gloom :
  There, sweet be my rest, till he bid me arise,
  To hail him in triumph descending the skies.

4 Who, would live alway away from his God ;
  Away from yon heaven, that blissful abode,
  Where the rivers of pleasure flow o'er the
      bright plains,
  And the noontide of glory eternally reigns ;

5 Where the saints of all ages in harmony **meet,**
The Saviour and brethren transported **to**
greet;
While the anthems of rapture unceasingly roll,
And the smile of the Lord is the feast of the
soul!

81. *A broken Heart I bring.* L. M.

1 O THOU that hearest when sinners cry;
Though all my crimes before thee lie;
Behold them not with angry look,
But blot their memory from thy book.

2 Create my nature pure within,
And form my soul averse to sin;
Let thy good Spirit ne'er depart,
Nor hide thy presence from my heart.

3 Though I have grieved thy Spirit, Lord,
Thy help and comfort still afford;
And let a wretch come near thy throne,
To plead the merits of thy Son.

4 A broken heart, my God, my King,
Is all the sacrifice I bring;
The God of grace will ne'er despise
A broken heart for sacrifice.

82. *I know that my Redeemer liveth.* L. M.

1 I know that my Redeemer lives;
What comfort this sweet sentence gives!
He lives, he lives, who once was dead,
He lives, my ever-living head.

2 He lives to bless me with his love,
He lives to plead for me above,
He lives my hungry soul to feed,
He lives to help in time of need.

3 He lives to grant me rich supply,
He lives to guide me with his eye,
He lives to comfort me when faint,
He lives to hear my soul's complaint.

4 He lives to silence all my fears,
He lives to wipe away my tears,
He lives to calm my troubled heart,
He lives, all blessings to impart.

5 He lives, all glory to his name!
He lives, my Jesus still the same;
O the sweet joy this sentence gives,
I know that my Redeemer lives!

83. *The faithful Appeal.* 7's.

1 SINNERS, turn, why will ye die?
God your Maker asks you why:
God, who did your being give,
Made you with himself to live;
He the fatal cause demands,
Asks the work of his own hands;
Why, ye thankless creatures, why
Will ye slight his love and die?

2 Sinners, turn, why will ye die?
God your Saviour asks you why:
He who did your souls retrieve,
Died himself that you might live.
Will you let him die in vain?
Crucify your Lord again?
Why, ye careless sinners, why
Will ye slight his grace, and die?

3 Sinners, turn, why will ye die?
God the Spirit asks you why:
He who all your lives hath strove,
Woo'd you to embrace his love:
Will ye not his grace receive?
Will ye still refuse to live?
O ye dying sinners, why,
Why will ye forever die?

84. *Importance of Time.* 8, 8, 6

1 Lo! on a narrow neck of land,
'Twixt two unbounded seas I stand,
  Yet how insensible!
A point of time, a moment's space,
Removes me to that heavenly place,
  Or shuts me up in hell!

2 O God! my inmost soul convert,
And deeply on my thoughtful heart
  Eternal things impress;
Give me to feel their solemn weight,
And save me ere it be too late,
  By thy almighty grace.

3 Before me place, in bright array,
The pomp of that tremendous day,
  When thou in clouds shalt come
To judge the nations at thy bar:
O tell me, Lord, shall I be there,
  To meet a joyful doom!

4 Be this my one great business here,
With holy joy and holy fear,
  To make my calling sure;
Assist, O Lord, a feeble worm,
Then shall I all thy will perform,
  And to the end endure.

85. *Christ our King.* L. M.

1 Jesus shall reign where'er the sun
  Does his successive journeys run ;
  His kingdom stretch from shore to shore,
  Till suns shall rise and set no more.

2 For him shall endless prayer be made,
  And endless praises crown his head ;
  His name, like sweet perfume, shall rise
  With every morning sacrifice.

3 People and realms of every tongue
  Dwell on his love with sweetest song ;
  And infant voices shall proclaim
  Their early blessings on his name.

4 Let every creature rise and bring
  Peculiar honors to our King ;
  Angels descend with song again,
  And earth repeat the loud amen.

86. *True Zeal.* C. M.

1 Zeal is that pure and heavenly flame
    The fire of love supplies ;
  While that which often bears the name
    Is self in a disguise.

2 True zeal is merciful and mild,
    Can pity and forbear;
The false is headstrong, fierce and wild,
    And breathes revenge and war.

3 Self may its poor reward obtain,
    And be applauded here;
But zeal the best applause will gain,
    When Jesus shall appear.

4 O Lord, the idol self dethrone,
    And from our hearts remove;
And let no zeal by us be shown,
    But that which springs from love.

87.   *Hope of Heaven.*   P. M.

1 RISE, my soul, and stretch thy wings,
    Thy better portion trace;
Rise from transitory things
    Towards heaven, thy native place;
Sun and moon, and stars decay,
    Time shall soon this earth remove;
Rise, my soul, and haste away
    To seats prepared above.

2 Rivers to the ocean run,
    Nor stay in all their course;

Fire, ascending, seeks the sun,
   Both speed them to their source :
So the soul that's born of God,
   Pants to view his glorious face,
Upward tends to his abode,
   To rest in his embrace.

3 Cease, ye pilgrims, cease to mourn ;
   Press onward to the prize ;
Soon our Saviour will return,
   Triumphant, in the skies :
Yet a season, and you know
   Happy entrance will be given ;
All our sorrows left below,
   And earth exchanged for heaven.

88.   *Confidence in God.*   C. M.

1 WHILE thee I seek, protecting Power !
   Be my vain wishes stilled ;
And may this consecrated hour
   With better hopes be filled.

2 Thy love the power of thought bestowed ;
   To thee my thoughts would soar :
Thy mercy o'er my life has flowed ;
   That mercy I adore.

3 In each event of life, how clear
    Thy ruling hand I see :
Each blessing to my soul most dear,
    Because conferred by thee.

4 In every joy that crowns my days,
    In every pain I bear,
My heart shall find delight in praise,
    Or seek relief in prayer.

5 When gladness wings my favoured hour,
    Thy love my thoughts shall fill ;
Resigned, when storms of sorrow lower,
    My soul shall meet thy will.

6 My lifted eye, without a tear,
    The gathering storm shall see ;
My steadfast heart shall know no fear ;
    That heart will rest on thee.

89.   *The Spirit's Influence.*   C. M.

1 COME, Holy Spirit, heavenly Dove,
    With all thy quickening powers ;
Kindle a flame of sacred love
    In these cold hearts of ours.

2 Look how we grovel here below,
  Fond of these trifling toys ;
Our souls can neither fly nor go
  To reach eternal joys.

3 In vain we tune our formal songs,
  In vain we strive to rise ;
Hosannas languish on our tongues,
  And our devotion dies.

4 Dear Lord ! and shall we ever live
  At this poor dying rate ?
Our love so faint, so cold to thee,
  And thine to us so great !

5 Come, Holy Spirit, heavenly Dove,
  With all thy quickening powers ;
Come, shed abroad a Saviour's love,
  And that shall kindle ours.

90.   *Leaning on Christ.*   L. P. M.

1 WHEN gathering clouds around I view
And days are dark, and friends are few,
On him I lean, who, not in vain,
Experienced every human pain,
He sees my wants, allays my fears,
And counts and treasures up my tears.

2 If aught should tempt my soul to stray
From heavenly virtue's narrow way,
To fly the good I should pursue,
Or do the sin I should not do ;
Still he, who felt temptation's power,
Shall guard me in that dangerous hour.

3 And O, when I have safely past
Through every conflict but the last,
Still, still unchanging, watch beside
My painful bed, for thou hast died ;
Then point to realms of cloudless day,
And wipe the latest tear away.

91. 7's.

"Redeeming the time, because the days are evil."—Eph. v. 16.

1 SINNER, rouse thee from thy sleep,
Wake, and o'er thy folly weep ;
Raise thy spirit dark and dead,
Jesus waits his light to shed.

2 Wake from sleep, arise from death,
See the bright and living path :
Watchful tread that path ; be wise,
Leave thy folly, seek the skies.

3 Leave thy folly, cease from crime,
From this hour redeem thy time ;

Life secure without delay,
Evil is the mortal day.

4 Be not blind and foolish still;
Called of Jesus, learn his will:
Jesus calls from death and night,
Jesus waits to shed his light.

92. *The Heavenly Rest.* L. M.

1 THINE earthly Sabbaths, Lord, we love,
But there's a nobler rest above:
Thy servants to that rest aspire
With ardent hope and strong desire.

2 There languor shall no more oppress;
The heart shall feel no more distress;
No groans shall mingle with the songs,
That dwell upon immortal tongues.

3 No gloomy cares shall there annoy,
No conscious guilt disturb our joy;
But every doubt and fear shall cease,
And perfect love give perfect peace.

4 When shall that glorious day begin,
Beyond the reach of death and sin;
Whose sun shall never more decline,
But with unfading lustre shine?

93. *Invitation to Praise.* S. M.

1 COME, ye who love the Lord,
     And let your joys be known ;
  Join in a song with sweet accord,
     And thus surround the throne.

2 Let those refuse to sing,
     Who never knew our God ;
  But servants of the heavenly King
     Should speak their joys abroad.

3 The men of grace have found
     Glory begun below ;
  Celestial fruits on earthly ground,
     From faith and hope may grow.

4 The hill of Zion yields
     A thousand sacred sweets,
  Before we reach the heavenly fields,
     Or walk the golden streets.

5 Then let our songs abound,
     And every tear be dry ;
  We're marching through Immanuel's ground
     To fairer worlds on high.

94. *The Burden of Sin.* L. M.

1 O THAT my load of sin were gone!
  O that I could at last submit,
At Jesus' feet to lay it down!
  To lay my soul at Jesus' feet!

2 Rest for my soul I long to find;
  Saviour of all, if mine thou art,
Give me thy meek and lowly mind,
  And stamp thine image on my heart.

3 Break off the yoke of inbred sin,
  And fully set my spirit free;
I cannot rest, till pure within,
  Till I am wholly lost in thee.

4 Fain would I learn of thee, my God,
  Thy light and easy burden prove;
Thy cross was stained with hallowed blood
  That I might taste thy dying love.

5 I would—but thou must give the power;
  My heart from every sin release;
Bring near, bring near the joyful hour,
  And fill me with thy perfect peace.

95. *Refuge for the Tempted.* 7's.

1 JESUS, lover of my soul,
    Let me to thy bosom fly ;
While the billows near me roll,
    While the tempest still is high !

2 Hide me, O my Saviour, hide,
    Till the storm of life is past;
Safe into the haven guide,
    O receive my soul at last !

3 Other refuge have I none,
    Hangs my helpless soul on thee ;
Leave, oh ! leave me not alone,
    Still support and comfort me !

4 All my trust on thee is stayed,
    All my help from thee I bring ;
Cover my defenceless head
    With the shadow of thy wing.

5 Plenteous grace with thee is found,
    Grace to pardon all my sins ;
Let the healing streams abound,
    Make and keep me pure within.

6 Thou of life the fountain art,
  Freely let me take of thee ;
Spring thou up within my heart,
  Rise to all eternity !

96.   8, 7.

" I have trusted in thy mercy ; my heart shall rejoice in thy salvation.—Ps. xiii. 5.

1 SAVIOUR, source of every blessing,
    Tune my heart to grateful lays ;
  Streams of mercy, never ceasing,
    Call for ceaseless songs of praise.

2 Teach me some melodious measure,
    Sung by raptured saints above ;
  Fill my soul with sacred pleasure,
    While I sing redeeming love.

3 Thou didst seek me when a stranger,
    Wandering from the fold of God ;
  Thou, to save my soul from danger,
    Didst redeem me with thy blood.

4 By thy hand restored, defended,
    Safe through life thus far I've come ;
  Safe, O Lord, when life is ended,
    Bring me to my heavenly home.

6

97.   *Rock of Ages.*   7's.

1 ROCK of Ages! cleft for me,
  Let me hide myself in thee;
  Let the water and the blood,
  From thy side, a healing flood,
  Be of sin the double cure,
  Save from wrath and make me pure.

2 Should my tears forever flow,
  Should my zeal no languor know,
  This for sin could not atone,
  Thou must save, and thou alone;
  In my hand no price I bring,
  Simply to thy cross I cling.

3 While I draw this fleeting breath,
  When mine eyelids close in death,
  When I rise to worlds unknown,
  And behold thee on thy throne,
  Rock of Ages! cleft for me,
  Let me hide myself in thee!

98.   *The Presence of Christ desired.*   L. M.

1 O THOU, to whose all-searching sight
  The darkness shineth as the light,
  Search, prove my heart, it pants for thee;
  Oh, burst these bonds, and set me free.

2 If in this darksome wild I stray,
  Be thou my light, be thou my way ;
  No foes. no violence I fear,
  No fraud, while thou, my God, art near.

3 When rising floods my soul o'erflow,
  When sinks my heart in waves of woe,
  Jesus, thy timely aid impart,
  To raise my head, and cheer my heart.

99. *The Lord is our Shepherd.* 11's.

1 THE Lord is our Shepherd, our guardian and
    guide;
  Whatever we want he will kindly provide,
  To sheep of his pasture his mercies abound,
  His care and protection his flock will surround.

2 The Lord is our Shepherd, what then shall
    we fear,
  What danger can move us, while Jesus is
    near ?
  Not when the time calls us to walk through
    the vale
  Of the shadow of death, shall our hearts ever
    fail.

3 Though afraid of ourselves to pursue the
    dark way,
Thy rod and thy staff be our comfort and stay,
For we know by thy guidance, when once it
    is past,
To a fountain of life it will bring us at last.

4 The Lord has become our salvation and song,
His blessings have followed us all our life long;
His name we will praise while he lends us
    our breath,
Be cheerful in life and be happy in death.

100.   11's.

"The rock of my strength, and my refuge, is in God."—Ps. lxii. 7.

1 How firm a foundation, ye saints of the Lord,
Is laid for your faith in his excellent word;
What more can he say than to you he hath
    said,
You who unto Jesus for refuge have fled:

2 Fear not, I am with thee, O be not dismayed,
I, I am thy God, and will still give thee aid;
I'll strengthen thee, help thee, and cause
    thee to stand,
Upheld by my righteous, omnipotent hand.

3 When through the deep waters I call thee to
    go,
  The rivers of woe shall not thee overflow;
  For I will be with thee, thy troubles to bless,
  And sanctify to thee thy deepest distress.

4 When through fiery trials thy pathway shall
    lie,
  My grace, all-sufficient, shall be thy supply;
  The flame shall not hurt thee, I only design
  Thy dross to consume, and thy gold to refine.

5 The soul that to Jesus has fled for repose,
  I will not, I will not desert to his foes;
  That soul, though all hell shall endeavour to
    shake,
  I'll never—no, never—no, never forsake.